Creations from the Heart

Creations from the Heart

Mable I. Cox

Mable I. Cox
Fort Washington, MD

Cover design by TLH Designs, Chicago, IL
Book design by Kingdom Living Publishing, Fort Washington, MD

For information about this book or to contact the author, write to:

Mable Cox
P.O. Box 441035
Fort Washington, Maryland 20744

You may also send the author an email message at:
beeyou5@gmail.com

Published by:
Mable Cox
Fort Washington, MD

Printed in the United States of America.

ISBN 978-0-615-52567-9

Dedication

God trusted two individuals to assist me in becoming the person I am today. God does not make mistakes and He knew, before my parents knew, how much love and joy I would bring them. These two people did what they could do to give me their love and the best that they felt life could offer.

I dedicate this book of poetry to my deceased parents, Milton and Ruth Cox. They inspired me and encouraged me in their own way. It was their love, prayers and examples that set the tone for me to continue to strive for all that God has for me.

Table of Contents

I.   Knowing God

II.   Love And Relationships

III. Life

IV. My Country, My Home And My Freedom

V. Etc.

VI. Short Story

Preface

I grew up alone. My parents were much older than my friends' parents and my sisters and brother were all older and starting their own lives. I spent most of my time talking to my father, listening to my mother telling me what and what not to do, reading and visiting the elderly with my parents. There, I heard all kinds of stories. The old folks loved to talk about their childhood and their young adult days. I listened as the older people expressed themselves and put life to whatever they talked about, whether it was growing up on the farm or in the city, whether it was feeding the pigs and chickens, or riding the city buses. They would talk about everything. They could talk for days and sometimes tell the same stories over and over. All they needed was someone willing to listen.

One of my favorite things was riding out Sunday evening with my parents. Sometimes daddy would tell me stories about his life or sometimes we would see someone at the store who would talk and talk and talk. I listened and most of the time I laughed. Sometimes I wondered if these stories were true or if the people created them as they talked. Later I found out that some of the stories were not true, but they were entertaining and animated. I grew older and found myself telling some of the same stories. I realized that not only could I tell them, but I could write them down for people to read, understand and relate.

I never knew I even had a desire to write until ninth grade. One day my journalism teacher had enough of my foolishness and gave me a choice to write a poem for the school newspaper or receive a detention. I wrote a poem for the school newspaper every week after that and became class poet of my senior class. Students and teachers admired my work.

Writing is so relaxing. It is a way to say what you want to say and how you want to say it. It almost comes naturally to me. In my writings, I examine who I am and what I want to be. I examine the real me inside of me. Hopefully you can identify. If not, just read and enjoy.

Knowing God

The Miracle

WHAT IS A MIRACLE? I USED TO SAY?
WHAT IS A MIRACLE? MAYBE, I WILL GET ONE TO-
DAY.

WHAT IS A MIRACLE? DO THEY STILL COME IN
THIS TIME?
WHAT IS A MIRACLE? WHEN WILL I GET MINE?

WHAT IS A MIRACLE? I NO LONGER SAY,
YOU SEE, GOD SAVED MY SOUL ONE DAY.

I AM A MIRACLE, CAN'T YOU SEE?
I AM ONE OF GOD'S MIRACLES, AND I WILL ALWAYS
BE.

<u>The Beginning</u>

IN THE BEGINNING GOD CREATED MAN,
HE GAVE HIM A WOMAN AND FINE LAND.

HE CALLED THIS MAN ADAM AND THE WOMAN
EVE,
AND GOD SUPPLIED THEM WITH THEIR EVERY
NEED.

THEY WERE GIVEN THE BEST THINGS GOD HAD,
BUT IN THE GARDEN, STOOD A DOSE OF THE BAD.

THE EVIL SERPENT THAT WAS NEAR THE TREE,
TEMPTED EVE WITH A FRUIT JUST LIKE HONEY
TEMPTS A BEE.

THIS WAS SOMETHING GOD TOLD THEM NOT TO
DO,
SO HE SENT THEM OUT OF THE GARDEN IN A
WORLD THAT WAS NEW.

STRANGE THINGS HAPPENED TO THEM EVERYDAY,
BUT GOD PROTECTED THEM IN HIS OWN WAY.

The Eagle

The Eagle Took off in Flight and as I Observed Him, I Saw:

His wings spreading wide, as if they were inviting the world to see the heavens.

His feathers fluttering, to beat off the sins of the world.

His head moving from side to side thinking of all of man's problems.

His eyes seeing the evilness and filth of the world.

His ears hearing the moans and cries of those that live for satan.

His body preparing to carry the whole world and her burdens.

His feet and toes stretching out to stand and step on satan's head.

The Eagle Took off in Flight and as I Observed Him, I Saw:

The heavens opening up to receive those who had accepted Jesus.

<u>the escape</u>

bound by prison cells.

bound by darkness.

bound by unbelief.

bound by doubt.

bound by fear.

but

there

is

LIGHT

peering through.

i see the light,

i can now escape

HELL.

i have found freedom and it is JESUS.

Things Are Looking Up!

THINGS ARE LOOKING UP!
CAN'T YOU SEE?
THINGS ARE WORKING OUT,
JUST FOR ME.

THINGS ARE LOOKING UP!
ISN'T IT GREAT?
THINGS ARE LOOKING UP,
I'M FINALLY GETTING A BREAK!

THINGS ARE LOOKING UP!
WHAT CAN I SAY?
THINGS ARE LOOKING UP, AND
TRUSTING GOD IS THE ONLY WAY.

Lord Hear Our Prayer

IN TIMES OF DISCOMFORT, PAIN AND GRIEF,
LORD, HEAR OUR PRAYERS AND GIVE US RELIEF.

IN LATE HOURS OF THE NIGHT,
LORD, HEAR OUR PRAYERS AND MAKE EVERY-
THING ALL RIGHT.

IN MOMENTS WHEN WE ARE IN FEAR,
LORD, HEAR OUR PRAYERS AND LET US KNOW
THAT YOU ARE NEAR.

LORD, WHEN ARE BODIES ARE LAID TO REST,
LET US BE REASSURED THAT WE DID OUR BEST.

i found Him

the morning was bright. the morning was clear. the morn-
ing was warm and peaceful. in the distance I heard a
voice calling me and in my heart, i knew it was He.

i tried not to answer. i tried not to listen. i tried to ignore
His voice, but in the distance you see, the voice still called
me, and in my heart i knew it was He.

i turned away. i walked on alone. i promised i would
answer one day, but still in the distance, i heard but a
whisper and this time the voice said to me, "deny yourself,
deny yourself and follow me."

i turned away and shed a tear. i turned and walked down
the road, but then i decided to go back and talk to Him. i
decided i would give Him my life.

now years have gone by and the world has changed. even
now, i am old and gray and my body is frail, but i still
belong to Him.

i fell in love that very day and yes i accepted Him.
yes, i found Him. yes, i found Him and i thank Him every-
day for choosing me.

In the Middle of the Night

IN THE MIDDLE OF THE NIGHT, HE CALLED ME.

IN THE MIDDLE OF THE NIGHT, HE WHISPERED MY NAME.

IN THE MIDDLE OF THE NIGHT, HE TOUCHED ME.

IN THE MIDDLE OF THE NIGHT, HE TOLD ME HE WOULD ALWAYS BE NEAR.

IN THE MIDDLE OF THE NIGHT, HE SAID HE WOULD NEVER LEAVE ME.

IN THE MIDDLE OF THE NIGHT, HE DRIED MY TEARS,

IN THE MIDDLE OF THE NIGHT, HE COMFORTED ME.

IN THE MIDDLE OF THE NIGHT, HE TOLD ME HE LOVED ME.

IN THE MIDDLE OF THE NIGHT, HE ASKED ME TO FOLLOW HIM.

IN THE MIDDLE OF THE NIGHT, I ACCEPTED HIM.

IN THE MIDDLE OF THE NIGHT, I FELT HIM NEAR ME,

IN THE MIDDLE OF THE NIGHT HE CLOTHED ME WITH HIS UNCONDITIONAL LOVE.

IN THE MIDDLE OF THE NIGHT, I ANSWERED GOD'S CALL.

AND, I WILL LIVE FOR HIM FOREVER.

Jesus, You Are Everything

Jesus, You are everything.
You are everything to me.

When I don't know where to turn,
You are there to guide me.

When my way gets dark,
You are my light.

When my body is wracked with pain,
You are my healer.

When my life seem to be so confusing,
You are my counselor.

When I am alone,
You are everything to me.

When problems seem unbearable,
You give me strength to go on.

When I feel like I can't make it anymore,
You remind me that You will never leave me nor forsake
me.

Jesus, You are everything to me,
Everything I need and everything I hope to be.

Bless This World

BLESS THIS WORLD, OH LORD I PRAY;
KEEP IT TOGETHER BY NIGHT AND DAY.

BLESS MY PEOPLE TO PROGRESS EVERYDAY;
OH LORD, SPEED US ON OUR WAY.

BLESS THE SICK LYING IN THE BED;
SOME NOT KNOWING WHETHER THEY ARE LIVING
OR DEAD.

BLESS THIS WORLD, OH LORD, AND PROTECT US
EVERYDAY;
IN YOUR OWN LOVING AND SWEET WAY.

The Faithless Life

DARKNESS, ISOLATION, CONFUSION,

LUST, PRIDE, GUILT, REJECTION,

PREJUDICE, JEALOUSLY, FEAR,

DRUGS, POVERTY, DEATH, HELL.

The Problem

SHE SMOKED

SHE DRANK

SHE LIED

SHE CRIED

SHE TOOK ADVANTAGE

OF OTHERS

SHE HATED

SHE FACED IT

SHE PRAYED

IT'S GONE!!!!!!!!!!!!!

Changes

Changes cause sadness.

Changes cause frustration.

Changes cause pain.

Changes cause stress.

Changes cause jealousy.

Changes cause low self esteem.

Change causes hatred.

Change causes death.

-BUT-

God changes not; He is everlasting.

Beauty Is the Morning

The sun is breaking through the sky.
The birds are singing.
Beauty Is The Morning.

The leaves on the trees are moving slowly.
The grass seems to lift itself towards the heavens.
Beauty Is The Morning.

The cars almost seem to stand at attention at the traffic
signals.
People are happily walking to work.
Beauty Is The Morning.

Doors are opening and closing.
Windows are being raised.
Beauty Is The Morning.

Breakfast is being served.
Newspapers are beginning to hit steps and front doors.
Beauty Is The Morning.

Neighbors are beginning to greet neighbors.
Students are beginning to board buses.
Beauty Is The Morning.

Telephones are ringing.
Computers are being turned on.
Beauty Is The Morning.

A new day is beginning.
The old has been forgotten.
Beauty Is The Morning.

Love

and Relationships

Thanksgiving Memories

THE TURKEY BAKED IN THE OVEN SO FINE,
AND ALL THE CHILDREN WAITED HUNGRILY IN
LINE.

THE VEGETABLES WERE DONE AND THE SAUCES
WERE MIXED,
AND ALL FIFTEEN PLATES WERE NEATLY FIXED.

SMILES AND LAUGHTER SHOWED ON ALL OUR
FACES,
AS SOON AS WE HEARD MAMA SAY, "TAKE YOUR
PLACES."

THE AROMA OF THE FOOD WOULD TEMPT US AS
DADDY WOULD PRAY,
IT SEEMED AS IF GOD ALWAYS GAVE HIM THE
RIGHT WORDS TO SAY.

BEING AROUND THE TABLE WITH MY FAMILY
MADE ME REMEMBER,
THE LOVE AND CARE WE SHARED IN NOVEMBER.

For God Supplied Us with a Mother

FOR GOD SUPPLIED US WITH A MOTHER,
SWEET, HUMBLE AND DIFFERENT FROM ANY
OTHER.

SHE TAUGHT US ALL RIGHT FROM WRONG
AND TO BE KIND, BRAVE AND STRONG.

FOR GOD SUPPLIED US WITH SUCH A LOVELY ONE,
TO SHOW AND TELL US ALL THE GREAT THINGS
SHE HAD DONE.

TIME WOULD COME WHEN WE WOULD SOME-
TIMES DISAGREE,
BUT OUR MOTHER WOULD HELP US UNDERSTAND
AND SEE.

FOR GOD SUPPLIED US WITH A MOTHER,
DEAR, INTELLIGENT AND ADMIRED BY OTHERS.

The Death of a Mother

Final!

The end.
No one similar to her and
No one to replace her.

Memories.
To have, hold and cherish,
They are never forgotten.

Void.
It will never be filled,
Full of pain, tears, fears and anger.

Loneliness.
Things remind me of her,
But she is not there.

The death of my mother!
My friend.

When She Died

WHEN SHE DIED, I CRIED.

WHEN SHE DIED, I WAS ALL ALONE.

WHEN SHE DIED, I WAS FRIGHTENED.

WHEN SHE DIED, I FELT EMPTY.

WHEN SHE DIED, I WAS IN PAIN.

WHEN SHE DIED, I WAS ANGRY.

WHEN SHE DIED, I HAD NOBODY TO TELL MY
SECRETS.

WHEN SHE DIED, I WANTED TO DIE.

WHEN SHE DIED, A PART OF ME DIED ALSO.

Mother's Last Words

I HAVE DONE FOR YOU ALL I CAN,
WORKED HARD, PUT CUTS AND SORES ON MY
HAND.

SCRUBBED THE WHITE MAN'S FLOORS,
SLEPT ON BENCHES AND CHAIRS OUTDOORS.

CARRIED YOU AND WORKED THE SAME TIME,
WALKED THE STREETS LOOKING THROUGH TRASH
AND BEGGING FOR QUARTERS, NICKELS AND
DIMES.

NOW I MUST LEAVE TO TAKE MY REST,
BE KIND, SWEET AND DO YOUR BEST.

DO NOT DROP OUT OF SCHOOL CHILD,
BUT STAY THERE AND LEARN A WHILE.

WHEN YOU HAVE CROSSED THE ROADS LIKE I
HAVE DONE,
YOU WILL FIND IT IS ALL WORK AND NO FUN.

AS THE MOTHER CLOSED HER EYES TIGHT,
THE CHID SAID, "WITH GOD'S HELP, I WILL BE ALL
RIGHT."

her

mama reared her.

society trained her.

streets taught her.

men took advantage of her.

life bored her.

death claimed her.

Out of All the Fellows in the World, I Chose You.

Out of all the fellows in the world, I chose you.

I prayed and asked my "Heavenly Father" for a man and, I chose you.

I searched and searched trying to find who God wanted me to have and, I chose you.

I was the one concerned about the children people bring into the world and, I chose you.

I wanted my children to have a spirit-filled father and, I chose you.

I, "Ms. Particular," who wanted the best out of life, I chose you.

I, who dreamed constantly of that beautiful house, beautiful wedding and beautiful life, I chose you.

I, who wanted that man just like my father, I chose you.

I, who wanted that Bible believing, God fearing man (one

who knew God and wanted to serve him), <u>I chose you.</u>

I looked and I searched and without seeking God first, <u>I chose you.</u>

I, who wanted desperately to stay in God's will, <u>I chose you.</u>

I disobeyed God, I walked out of His will and, <u>I chose you.</u>

Out of all the fellows in the world, God had "one" just for me, and <u>I chose you.</u>

My Man

MY MAN IS A VERY BRAVE MAN,
AND HE DOES FOR ME ALL HE CAN.

HE HAS HELPED ME MAKE IT THROUGH THE DAY,
IN HIS WARM AND SWEET WAY.

I MET MY MAN ONE DAY IN THE STREET,
AS I STOOD THERE BEGGING FOR FOOD TO EAT.

HE TOOK ME IN AND HE FED ME WELL,
OH, I KNOW HE LOVES ME, I CAN TELL.

NEVER HAS HE EVER RAISED HIS VOICE AT ME,
HE TREATS ME GENTLE AS CAN BE.

NO ONE CAN EVER TAKE HIM AWAY,
BECAUSE THIS MAN KEPT ME FROM RUNNING
ASTRAY.

HOW I LOVE HIM EVERYDAY OF MY LIFE,
AND I AM THANKFUL THAT I AM HIS WIFE.

THIS MAN HAS DONE SO MUCH FOR ME,
FOR WITHOUT HIM, ONLY GOD KNOWS WHERE I
WOULD BE.

I Remember

I REMEMBER YOUR SWEET AND UNDERSTANDING
LOVE,
THAT SEEMED AS IF IT DRIPPED DOWN FROM
HEAVEN ABOVE.

I REMEMBER YOUR LIPS CLOSE TO MINE,
OH, DARLING, YOU TREATED ME SO KIND.

I REMEMBER THE SWEET THINGS YOU WHIS-
PERED IN MY EAR,
WHEN I WAS NEAR YOU, I HAD NOTHING TO FEAR.

I REMEMBER THE WALKS WE USED TO TAKE,
AND ALL THE IMMATURE THINGS WE USED TO
MAKE.

I REMEMBER MOST OF ALL THE LOVE WE USED TO
SHARE,
BUT NOW IT HAS GROWN OLD AND VERY BARE.

YOU HAVE FOUND ANOTHER TO TAKE MY PLACE,
AND LEFT ME WITH WORRIES AND BURDENS TO
FACE.

ALL I HAVE ARE MEMORIES OF YOU TO HOLD,
ONES I CHERISHED DAILY THAT HAVE NOW
TURNED OLD.

YOUR NEW LOVE WILL HAVE THE LOVE WE ONCE
HAD,
SHE WILL BE SHARING YOUR LOVE, THE GOOD
TIMES AND THE BAD.

START A NEW LIFE AND NO MATTER WHAT YOU DO,
ALWAYS REMEMBER, I ONCE LOVED YOU.

Close to Me

THERE IS A MAN SO BIG AND STRONG,
WHO HAS NEVER DONE ME ANY HARM.

HOW I WISH HIM TO BE CLOSE TO ME,
LIKE THE BEES THAT SURROUND THE HONEY
TREE.

HE STAYS NEAR AND LIVES IN MY HEART,
AND NEVER DOES HE SEEM TO DEPART.

HE IS THE MAN OF ALL MY DREAMS,
NO MATTER HOW HARD IT MAY SEEM.

WITH ALL YOUR TALENTS AND DEGREES,
I FEEL YOU STILL HAVE AN UNFULFILLED NEED.

I LOVE YOU, AND I WANT YOU CLOSE TO ME
LIKE THE SEED THAT PRODUCES THE APPLE TREE.

WITHOUT YOU WHAT COULD I DO,
FOR HEAVEN KNOWS, I LOVE YOU.

Your Everlasting Vows

PEACE GO WITH YOU AS YOU START YOUR NEW
LIFE,
YES, YOU ARE NOW A HUSBAND, AND SHE IS YOUR
WIFE.

YOU HAVE TAKEN THE GREATEST VOWS OF ALL,
WHETHER YOU OBSERVE THEM AS LARGE OR
SMALL.

IN GOD'S EYES YOUR VOWS ARE NEVER UNDONE,
FOR YOU HAVE BEEN JOINED TOGETHER AND NOW
ARE ONE.

HARDSHIPS AND STRUGGLES WILL SOMETIMES
STAND IN YOUR WAY,
BUT OBEY GOD AND ALWAYS PRAY.

NOW AS I CLOSE WITH WORDS OF LOVE FOR YOUR
MARRIAGE IN MY HEART,
ALWAYS REMEMBER YOU ARE HERS AND SHE IS
YOURS UNTIL DEATH DO YOU PART.

Friend

YOU FOUND ME WHEN I WAS LOW,
YOU BENT DOWN AND LIFTED ME UP.
YOU LISTENED WHEN I TALKED,
YOU MOANED WHEN I CRIED.

YOU UNDERSTOOD ME,
YOU TAUGHT ME HOW TO ANALYZE MY DIFFICULT
PROBLEMS.
YOU ASSISTED ME IN FRIGHTENING SITUATIONS,
YOU GUIDED ME IN THE RIGHT DIRECTION.

YOU INQUIRED ABOUT MY PAINFUL EXPERIENCES
I NEVER ACCEPTED,
YOU EXEMPLIFIED THE JOY AND BEAUTY OF
SURVIVAL.

Don't Underestimate God's Greatest Gift

WHAT IS GOD'S GREATEST GIFT?
I AM SURE EVERYONE HAS HIS/HER OWN ANSWER,
BUT TO ME, IT IS A FRIEND.

A FRIEND
IS OFTEN TAKEN FOR GRANTED, UNDERESTIMAT-
ED AND SOMETIMES
MISUNDERSTOOD.

A FRIEND
IS ONE WHO TELLS YOU THE TRUTH, LOVES YOU
WHEN YOU FEEL NO ONE ELSE DOES, IS THERE
WHEN NO ONE ELSE IS THERE AND WILL BE WITH
YOU NO MATTER WHAT.

A FRIEND
IS A SPECIAL GIFT, WRAPPED, EMBROIDERED AND
PRESENTED FROM GOD'S OWN HANDS.

A FRIEND
UNDERSTANDS, CARES, HEARS WHEN NO ONE
ELSE LISTENS, CRIES WITH YOU AND FOR YOU
AND WANTS THE BEST FOR YOU WHEN YOU DON'T
WANT THE BEST FOR YOURSELF.
WHAT IS GOD'S GREATEST GIFT?

EVERYONE HAS HIS/HER OWN ANSWER
BUT TO ME, IT IS YOU BECAUSE YOU ARE MY BEST
FRIEND AND WITHOUT YOU, MY LIFE WOULD BE
DIFFERENT.

YOU ARE TRULY A GIFT FROM GOD AND I DO NOT
UNDERESTIMATE YOUR FRIENDSHIP.

THANKS FOR BEING THERE AND MOST OF ALL
THANKS FOR BEING MY FRIEND.

Life

L I F E

Let

It

Forever

Envelope Mankind.

The Eye in the Midst of the Tunnel

Look inside my heart
And see
The love I have to offer

Look inside my heart
And see
The love that I am afraid to give

Look inside my heart
And see
The dreams that I cannot share

Look inside my heart
And see
The words that are difficult to utter

Look inside my heart
And see
How badly I want you in my life

Look inside my heart
And see
The chains that continue to bind me

Look inside my heart
And see
The pain that still exist

Look inside my heart
And see
The real me desperately trying to get out

Look inside my heart
And see
An abundance of unknown emotions

Look inside my heart
And direct me to the avenues of freedom

Difficult

MY MIND IS FILLED WITH THOUGHTS THAT I CAN-
NOT MAKE KNOWN.

MY EYES ARE FILLED WITH VISIONS THAT I CAN-
NOT EXPLAIN.

MY EARS HAVE CAPTURED SOUND THAT I CANNOT
HEAR.

MY MOUTH IS FILLED WITH WORDS THAT I CAN-
NOT SPEAK.

MY HEART IS FILLED WITH LOVE THAT I CANNOT
EXPRESS.

MY HANDS ARE FILLED WITH STRENGTH THAT I
CANNOT USE.

MY BODY IS FILLED WITH GESTURES THAT I CAN-
NOT SHOW.

MY LIFE IS FILLED WITH HAPPINESS THAT I CAN-
NOT FIND.

My Country,
My Home
and
My Freedom

The Letter

THIS COUNTRY ENVELOPED ME.

IT SEALED ME WITH AN ENCLOSED CIRCLE.

IT DATED ME WITH A TIME THAT WAS STOLEN
FROM MY PEOPLE.

IT STAMPED ME WITH A LABEL MARKED ABUSED.

IT SENT ME TO THE FAR SHORES OF THE
UNKNOWN.

IT DELIVERED ME TO AN UNKNOWN ADDRESS.

IT TORE ME OPEN AND STRIPPED ME OF MY
DIGNITY.

IT NEVER RETURNED ME TO MY HOMELAND.

Africa

LAND OF BEAUTIFUL BROWN SKINNED PEOPLE,
AFRICA.

LAND OF POWER, INTELLIGENCE AND WEALTH,
AFRICA.

LAND OF VIGOR, WARMTH AND LOVE,
AFRICA.

LAND THAT WILL NO LONGER BE CONTAMINATED
WITH HATE,
AFRICA.

LAND THAT WILL ONE DAY EXHIBIT FREEDOM AND
EQUALITY,
AFRICA.

LAND THAT BELONGS TO ME,
AFRICA.

My Tribute To
Dr. Martin Luther King, Jr.
(A Child's Perspective)

I was born in a small town in North Carolina and I remember those "white" and "colored" signs. I asked my father why those signs were there and he said because the colored people couldn't sit with the white folks. I accepted that and didn't ask any more questions.

Two month passed and one night while looking at our black and white television, I saw you. I saw you marching. I saw you singing and I heard you talking about civil rights. I saw you and other people being kicked, dragged and beaten.

I do not remember asking my father any more questions, but I am sure he explained to me what was going on. I remember going to bed thinking about that awful scene. Then I heard some terrible news. Several months later, I heard you were shot and later died. People in the community cried and they talked about your great works.

But guess what, Dr. King? Those signs went down. The schools were integrated. They have finally decided to celebrate your birthday. I was fortunate than a lot of people because I did not go through as much, but I am not

foolish. I saw and still see prejudiced people. I still see
people discriminated against. Racism is still around and
it is still destroying innocent people.
Dr. King, you helped me. You taught me a sense of pride.
You taught me that God made no mistake in COLORING
my skin. I am proud of my heritage and my race.

Dr. King, thanks for allowing God to use you. Thanks for
helping us understand. Thanks for teaching me about
nonviolence. Thanks for fighting for me. Dr. King, remem-
ber this: If you would not have taken a stand for equality,
I don't know where I would be.

Thanks, Dr. King. Thanks for the sacrifice.

African Americans

Marcus Garvey, Martin Luther King and Malcolm X,
Are African Americans who should always get respect.

Their speeches roamed the world day by day,
And told African Americans that togetherness was the
only way.

Langston Hughes, Countee Cullen and Claude McKay,
Wrote their poems and short stories day by day.

They expressed themselves in lines that were clear and
brief,
And when reading their works, African Americans got a
stronger belief.

Zora Hurston, Chester Himes and Willis Richardson pre-
sented scenes so great,
And told African Americans no longer to wait.

James Weldon Johnson's love for African Americans still
ring,
When we stand to recall <u>Lift Ev'ry Voice and Sing</u>.

African Americans, standing in the dark is no longer for
us,
But togetherness is a must.

ETC.

I Did Not Know

I DID NOT KNOW THE EFFECTS OF THAT SMALL
PILL,
I DID NOT KNOW THAT IT WOULD KILL.

I DID NOT KNOW THIS WOULD HAPPEN TO ME,
I WAS ALWAYS CAUTIOUS, CAN'T YOU SEE.

I DID NOT KNOW THAT I WOULD DESTROY
SOMEONE'S BROTHER,
I DID NOT KNOW THAT I WOULD DESTROY MY
MOTHER.

I DID NOT KNOW THAT TAKING DRUGS WAS A
DANGEROUS GAME,
I JUST THOUGHT IT WOULD GIVE ME PLEASURE
AND INSTANT FAME.

I DID NOT KNOW THAT I WOULD SPEND MY LIFE
STARING AT THESE HALLS,
I DID NOT KNOW THAT I WOULD SPEND MY NIGHT
ALMOST CLIMBING THESE WALLS.

I DID NOT KNOW THAT I WOULD END UP LIKE
THIS,
I DID NOT KNOW THAT MY NAME WOULD BE ON A
DEATH'S LIST.

I DID NOT KNOW THE EFFECTS OF THAT SMALL
PILL,
I DID NOT KNOW THAT IT WOULD MAKE ME KILL.

The Teenage Mother

Moments of pleasure put me here
Thinking I was in love put me here.
Following the in-crowd put me here.
Desiring to experience life put me here.
Wanting to be an adult put me here.
Needing someone to love me for me put me here.
Never wanting to be alone put me here.
Thinking I could take care of myself put me here.
Becoming interested in the wrong individual put me here.
Going to the wrong places with the wrong people put me
here.
Not listening to others put me here.
Believing it would never happen to me put me here.
Knowing I had it all under control put me here.
Hanging out in the streets and doing my own thing put
me here.
I am here, I am a teenage mother.

The Rattlesnake
(A Child's Poem)

I ADMIRED THE RATTLESNAKE,
I LIKED THE WAY HE LOOKED,
I LIKED THE WAY HE SMELLED,
I LIKED THE WAY HE LOOKED AT ME.

I ADMIRED THE RATTLESNAKE,
I LIKED THE WAY HE HISSED,
I LIKED THE WAY HE CRAWLED,
I LIKED THE WAY HE LOOKED AT ME.

I ADMIRED THE RATTLESANKE,
I LIKED HIS TINY MOUTH,
I LIKED THE SLENDER TONGUE,
I LIKED THE WAY HE LOOKED AT ME.

I ADMIRED THE RATTLESNAKE,
I LIKED THE WAY HE MOVED HIS BODY CLOSER TO
MY FEET,
UNTIL SUDDENLY, SUDDENLY, HE BIT ME!
I NO LONGER LIKE THE WAY HE LOOKED AT ME.

SHORT STORY

Distant Lover

January 15, 1998, was the day Jesse came home from the big fight. He was happy and sad at the same time. He was happy because Buster had finally won a fight after five years of going to the gymnasium and sad because Tiger died that night. Tiger was Jesse's best friend. He loved her and thanked God for the day he met her.

Jesse was at the recreational center with his niece when he looked across the pool and saw this beautiful woman sitting in a lime green recliner not far from the lifeguard. Jesse grabbed his niece's hand and ran toward this gorgeous young woman. As he got closer to her, he immediately realized that she was a mature "sophisticated lady." Her body screamed twenty-five. She had curly black hair, her eyes were the same shade of the water in the pool and her lips were small and appeared ready for a kiss. She was the prettiest woman he had ever seen. Jesse just could not keep his eyes off her. After looking at her for almost ten minutes, he introduced himself to her. Before she could give her name, he said, "How old are you?"

Tiger look astonished, smiled, and said, "I am forty-five and how old are you?" He shouted out, "Age does not make a difference. Tell me that you will take me home and be mine forever." Tiger laughed and said, "Oh, you are young enough to be my child, but they say younger men are better." Jesse smiled and said, "I have to take my niece home, but I cannot leave without getting that telephone number." Tiger said, "Okay," and gave him her name and number. She asked him his niece's name. He yelled, "Monica," then he said, "I have to go, I will see you later pretty lady, and I will call you."

Smiling to herself, Tiger walked home. She thought, "I had a conversation with this young man and believe it or not he is cute and truly something to think about late tonight." She laughed to herself and said, "I am sure he won't call me."

After shopping, buying groceries, and stopping by the video store, Tiger arrived home. She opened the door just in time to hear this deep voice on the answering machine. She smiled and said, "I don't believe that young man called me." She rewound the machine and listened to five calls from that young man she met at the recreational center. She could not believe that this young man had called and left his name after every message.

Tiger went in the kitchen and prepared her meal. She unplugged the machine and turned the television on. Dinner was short – a hotdog, fries, and cola. While she was sitting there, shaking ketchup on her fries and thinking about the events of the day, she heard a knock on her door. Tiger listened, got up slowly, and went in the direction of the door. As she approached the door, she asked, "Who's there?" "Jesse, the guy you met at the rec. center." Tiger was astonished. She said, "What are you doing here." Jesse said, "Technology is awesome. I found your address in the computer. It was no way I was going to let a pretty woman like you go. I am outside, it is not cold out here, but I wouldn't mind coming in to get out of the sun." Tiger could not believe her ears. She said, "I don't know you. I will say, you are a cute young man. By the way, why are you here?" Jesse replied that he wanted to talk to her briefly. Tiger laughed to herself and said, "I know I am taking a chance."

She opened the door and said, "Come in." Jesse walked in and said, "Well, you didn't call me back, so I tracked you down. I have a couple of friends who live in this area also."

Tiger was shocked. She did not know what to say. She thought, "What have I done letting this young guy in my house?" She asked Jesse if he wanted something to eat. He said he was not hungry, but just interested in getting to know her better. Tiger asked Jesse if he looked women up on a regular basis. She asked him if he was okay or if he was some kind of freak. Jesse smiled. He told her he was only a freak for love and good looking women. He said he knew she was older, and he knew what he said would sound childish, but he was in love with her. Tiger told him that line truly told her how young he was. Tiger laughed and told him it was probably time for him to go. Jesse told her he would, but he wanted her to know that he had met the woman that he had been dreaming of for years. He told her he was in love.

Tiger looked at him and said, "You don't know how uncomfortable you make me feel. Please leave. I am so sorry I let you in my house. I am not that kind of person, but please leave." Tiger said, "I am old enough to be your mother."

Jesse said he did not care. He said he just wanted to be with her and if she said it was okay, he would spend the rest of his life with her. Jesse told her that he was not making the money that he should be making. He said he was a trainer down at the gym and once his guy won a couple of fights, he would definitely be on the map.

Tiger looked at him and smiled. She opened the door even wider and asked him to leave. She said, "Slow down honey, you don't know me." She said, "But for the rest of the time I have left on this earth, I promise you we can be friends. Leave! Call me later, and we will talk."

Jesse did not move. He asked her what she meant by that statement. Tiger told Jesse that she had leukemia and the doctor had given her a year to live. She said, "Well as of today, I only have six months to go." She said, "So you understand why I don't want any funny business. I need this time to myself. Please leave, for the last time."

Jesse looked at Tiger and began to cry. Tiger looked at him more astonished now than before. She asked him if he was okay and if he had escaped from some institution. She said that she needed to call the police. She told him that she did not want any trouble. She also told him that her neighbors watched her daily. She assured him that someone was watching both of them as they were talking.

Jesse said, "You don't understand. I know I am twenty-five, but believe it or not you are the woman I have been looking for all my adult life. When I saw you today, my world and the things I want to do in life got brighter and brighter. I need a woman like you. Please don't shut me out of your life. Spend those six months with me. Let me love you and hold you until God takes you home. I want to be your air, your comfort, you anchor. I just want to be in your life from this day until the end. I felt so warm inside when I saw you. Your eyes, your lips, your face, your body, everything about you made me happy. You make me feel like a man. Love at first sight really happened to me. I have had girlfriends and lovers. I have even been engaged and called it off because I was not in love. You are what I have been waiting for all my life. I have made a commitment to myself and God that I would never cheat on my wife, but if I were married and feeling like I am now about you, I would have to leave her. Tiger, I know I have talked a long time, but I can't just go. You have to tell me that you will at least give me one hour, one evening or one night, to be with you and enjoy all that you have to offer."

Tiger looked at Jesse and said, "Do you know I am old enough to be your mother? Jesse, I am forty-five years old. I am a widow with no children. I am quickly dying with leukemia. What do you want from me? Jesse, what can I offer you. I can't even offer you a life insurance policy."

Jesse looked at Tiger and said, "I want none of that. Tiger, I want you. I know you are old enough to be my mother, but aren't you aware of older women and younger men relationships. Tiger please don't let age be a hindrance to something that I promise you will be beautiful in the end. I can see it in your eyes. We both feel this. Tiger, I beg you, don't let this go." Tiger looked at Jesse and said, "Sure I am aware of older women/younger men relationships and vice versa, but Jesse I am older than you. I am sure there is a younger pretty little thing out there that you could spend the rest of your life with. Sweetheart, I am dying. Did you hear me when I said that? My disease is terminal. I have already planned my funeral. This was not a part of it. I have six months to live. What can we do in six months? As soon as it starts, it will be over. I don't have long to spend with you even if I felt this was worthwhile."

Jesse smiled and said, "It is worthwhile. Tiger, I love you. Tiger, please tell me that you feel the same way and if you don't I will understand. I will leave and never bother you again. Tiger, I am waiting for your answer. Do you feel the same way?"

Tiger said, "Well Jesse, you are a nice fellow and let me not waste time. I don't know what I am feeling. I just met you. I don't know what it is, but I do feel something, but..."

Jesse stopped her and said, "But nothing, I love you." Jesse grabbed her and kissed her. Tiger looked at Jesse and told him to go home. Jesse smiled and told Tiger he was an adult. He was not a child and he knew what they were feeling was real. Tiger smiled and said, "Since you are so much of an adult, go home and call me in the morning. If we both feel something then, we will talk about it. I promise." Jesse smiled and left. He told her that he would call her in the morning.

Jesse left and Tiger was puzzled. She could not believe this man. She was flattered by what he had said. She just could not believe this was happening. She felt something too. How could she tell this child that what she was feeling was similar? Tiger laughed to herself. She walked into the living room and sat and sat. She thought about Jesse and wondered how could this be? All her life, she had wished and hoped for another man after Wilbur's death. She loved him with all of her being. She could not believe that she was feeling something for someone at this stage of her life. She was dying. Jesse was twenty years younger. Tiger smiled, got up, and went in her bedroom. She looked at herself in the mirror and said, "I must be crazy; I am going to bed."

Around two in the morning Tiger awakened in a deep sweat. She was too embarrassed to even think about her dream. She could not believe what she had dreamed. How did Jesse get in her dream? She sat up in her bed and thought about Jesse. She got a drink of water that she had on her nightstand and just thought and thought. Finally she said, "I got to talk to this boy. This is weird." Tiger laid back down and drifted off to sleep again.

Morning came too soon for Tiger. Jesse called Tiger and asked if he could move in with her or if she wanted to move in with him. He said he did not understand her illness, but he wanted her to spend the rest of her time with him. Tiger told Jesse that he was very aggressive with his plan. She told him that he had no right to make that decision without asking her. Tiger admitted that she was still feeling something, but if he would give her his address, she would come by and talk. Jesse apologized and gave her his address. He also told her how to get there. Tiger told him that as soon as she dressed she would be there. Jesse told her that he could not wait.

Jesse's place was great. Everything was neat, comfortable, and cozy. It was a bit small, but it was okay. Immediately Tiger could tell a lot about him. He was clean and organized. Tiger was so happy to see Jesse, but she would not let him know that. She remembered her mother telling her to never let a man know how you really feel in the beginning. She did not know where this feeling was coming from or what was happening. She thought about her mother, her friends, and her late husband and wondered what they would say about her dating or possibly considering spending her last days with this young boy. She smiled to herself and wondered if this was another stage of her sickness. She always wanted children, but never conceived. She wondered if she was looking at Jesse as the child she never had. She just could not understand what was happening. There was a part of her that felt ashamed because of the age difference and there was a part of her that did not care. She thought and thought, but like Jesse she was so happy. She wondered if this boy was telling the truth or if this was one of his lines he used on every woman. Even

being in Jesse's house made her feel loved and safe; she felt
like Jesse adored her. Jesse asked her what she was think-
ing. He said that she walked in looked around and seemed
as if she had gone in some kind of trance. He asked her if
she was okay. Tiger smiled and said, "Jesse, I don't know
what's going on. I feel like I am dreaming. Worse yet, I feel
like some school girl. I can't resist this feeling any longer. I
dare not share my dream with you, but I would love for it
to come true." Tiger told Jesse that she only had six months
to live and whatever they decided, she did not feel any pain
could be as worse as her life ending. Tiger told Jesse that
she thought she loved him also. She said, "Jesse this is so
strange. You are a young man, we have not had anytime to-
gether, and we have not talked about life, what you want to
do with the rest of your life after I leave you, what we want,
what our dreams are, or anything. This seems so right and
so strange. I thought I would never say this to any man,
but I want you to move in with me. I don't have long, but
if you would have me the way you say you want me, then I
want to spend the rest of my days with you." Tiger laughed.
Jesse asked her what was wrong. She said, "Marriage is an
honorable thing. I guess I can't mess it up. Either we get
married or we move on." In her mind, Tiger figured that
was her way out. Jesse immediately said, "Set the date."

Jesse grabbed her and held her so tightly. Tiger loved
every minute of him holding her near him. At that point,
Tiger knew she had made the right decision. She asked him
how was Saturday. She told him that she could talk to her
pastor and was almost sure that they could take their vows
that morning. Jesse agreed. He kissed Tiger. Jesse jumped
up and down, ran around the room, hugged Tiger and told
her that she had made the right decision.

Tiger smiled and told him she was leaving to make the necessary arrangements. As she opened the door, Jesse said, "Call the pastor." Tiger could not believe that she was making such a swift decision. As she picked up the telephone, she realized that she did not know anything about this boy, whom she was planning on marrying. She called Jesse and asked him to tell her something about his life.

Jesse told her that he was the oldest of five children. He said at age fifteen, both of his parents and his younger sister were killed in a car accident. He said that it was an icy morning and they were taking his sister to daycare. Some man slid into them and knocked them in an embankment. No one ever found the person who hit them. He told her that he and his three brothers went to live with his aunt. She was a school teacher and after being there two years, she died of cancer. He said that no one knew she was sick. She went to work every day and took care of them. He said that she was the nicest aunt. She really loved all of them. Her husband had died five years earlier of a heart attack. She had a hard time dealing with his death, but he felt that their living with her helped her a lot. Jesse said he stayed in the house and took care of his three brothers until his father's brother came and got them.

Jesse said he finished high school and went to a community college. He graduated in graphic design, but he fell in love with boxing. He boxed in high school and he was always at the community center watching the guys box. After jumping in the ring and getting beaten, he decided that boxing was not for him, but maybe he could manage a boxer. He said his parents invested their money and all of them received a large amount after they died. So he invested some of his in boxing. He said he had two fighters.

One was okay, but the other one, Buster, would bring him an additional nest egg. Tiger laughed and said, "Whatever makes you happy." She asked about his three brothers. He told her that they were living in New Jersey. Tiger decided to stop with the questions. He told her that he had several friends, a few cousins, and a couple of adopted nieces in town and that he was sure she would meet all of them.

By midnight, Jesse had moved everything he wanted to take to Tiger's house. They both were tired. Tiger had made all of the arrangements and they were scheduled to be married Saturday. All Tiger could think about was one more day and then she would be Mrs. Jesse Rogers. While she was thinking about that, she called Jesse in to tell him something about herself. He was exhausted, but willing to listen.

Tiger told Jesse that she did not know her mother. She was adopted. She said that her adopted mother always told her that her mother was in the same city and that she had passed her on the streets. Tiger said after hearing that, she used to look at women who had her complexion and wonder if one of them was her mother. She said that her adopted mother told her that she nicknamed her Tiger because she always called cats "tigers." Tiger laughed and said what a silly reason. She said she grew up with that name and that few people really know that her name is Evelyn. She said she really loves the name Tiger. Jesse and Tiger both laughed. She told him that she had a happy childhood, but after finding out she was adopted, it bothered her. She was so happy that the Anderson's adopted her, but she could never understand a mother giving up her child. She told Jesse maybe that is why she never had children. Jesse held her closely as she talked about that. He could still see the hurt in Tiger's eyes. He told her to continue with her story. She said she was given everything. Her mom adored her. She went to the best schools and colleges and her parents were proud of her. She told him that it just didn't seem fair that her life was going to be over soon. Jesse said that maybe they could go to other doctors and specialist. Tiger told him that she and her mother had found the best doctors. She had resolved within herself that her time had expired. A tear rolled down Jesse's eyes. She wiped it away and told him that she had accepted her death and that she would be okay. She told him that she wanted him to find another woman after her death, but realized that this union/marriage must have been destined from the beginning. Jesse smiled and told her these would be the happiest six months she would ever have.

Tiger told her mother about Jesse. Her mother asked all of the mother questions. Where did you meet him? Do you know anything about him? Do you know he is much younger than you? Where is he going to live? Does he have a job? Are you signing your house and money over to him? After Tiger answered all of the questions, her mother was silent for about twenty minutes. Finally she told her that she wanted her happy. She told her that if this would make her happy, then she was happy for her. She said that she wanted to meet the man that caused her to change her whole life pattern. Tiger promised her that she would meet him soon. Her mother reminded her of how her father gave Wilbur the third degree. She said that if he was still alive she was sure Jesse would have a hard time. They both laughed and Tiger thanked her for being so understanding and let Jesse talk to her on the telephone. Jesse told her how much he loved her daughter and that neither she nor Tiger would ever regret the day he came in their lives. The mother reminded him of how much she loved her daughter and that her first cousin was a policeman. They both laughed. She told Jesse to take care of her daughter and for both of them to come by often and visit her in the nursing home.

Saturday was the shortest and longest day coming. Tiger and Jesse married after two hours of marriage counseling from the pastor. The pastor was a bit shocked too, but he reminded them of their commitment to God first and then to each other. Their honeymoon was spent in the hotel across town. Jesse decided that he did not want to travel far. He wanted to start the honeymoon real soon. Tiger knew that day that she had made the right decision.

Jesse would not allow Tiger to do anything. All he wanted was for her to be his lady. Tiger loved everything Jesse did. He often told her to just leave the pampering to him. He was truly Tiger's dream come true. He was the perfect husband for her. Tiger knew she had everything. She would often remind Jesse of her disease. He would always tell her that he was praying for more months to be with her. Sometimes she would even hide her pain because she wanted to be so right for him. Jesse would always tell her that no matter what happened he would always be there.

Her mother loved Jesse. She was happy for both of them. Jesse spent time with Tiger's mother. He took her out shopping while Tiger relaxed. Tiger's mother told Jesse that she could not have a better son-in-law. Everything was working out great. Not only did Tiger's mother adore him, but so did her friends. Tiger's mother invited all of the nursing home women to meet him. She told him that she was not going to introduce him to the staff because they were too young. They both laughed. Most of the women declared that they would find them a younger man. Jesse laughed and laughed. One woman asked him about his sex life. He knew not to answer that question. They all applauded Tiger for picking such a good looking young man. Tiger reminded all of them that he was happily married. Those old women were something else, but he loved spending time with them.

Jesse loved his job and he was determined to make his boxer the greatest boxer ever. Buster was an outstanding boxer. He just needed someone to care for him and let him know he was important. Buster was eighteen, had a rough childhood, never knew his father, and was number five of ten children. Jesse cared for Buster and treated him like a little brother. Tiger liked Buster. He was a decent young man. She decided that if Buster was Jesse's friend, he was her friend. She did not like boxing. She thought it was a rough sport, but if that was what Jesse liked, she would be there for him. She learned very early to cheer Buster on. She was at every fight. Tiger started suggesting different styles of boxing shorts Buster would wear. Even though the locker room smelled of sweat and she held her nose when she walked in, she was there to give Buster his little pep talk. Buster loved both of them. He often told Tiger that Jesse was a much better trainer after she came into his life. Tiger would always tell Buster that he always knew what to say to women. She invited Buster over for dinner and he was always in the basement with Jesse discussing boxing moves.

Jesse adored the ground Tiger walked on. He knew she was sick, but he asked Tiger numerous times if they could have a baby. Tiger would laugh and remind him of the six months she had to live. She often told him that she was in her fifth month and quickly slipping into her fourth. Tiger would tell him no, but Jesse would also tell her he wanted a part of her forever. Tiger would also explain to him that she was forty-five years old. She told him that her biological clock was completely stuck. She would joke and say that the hands could not move. She told Jesse that that was one thing she could not give him. She was concerned about her health and the baby's health. He would walk away sad, but quickly turn and say that he was thankful that God loved him enough to give him her.

Tiger had a doctor's appointment. It seemed as if they were every three weeks. She would go faithfully and talk to her doctor about her death. He had recommended a thera- pist, but she said she would rather talk to him. Dr. Robertson and Tiger talked about everything from her sex life with Jesse to the flowers she had planted in her yard. She told her doctor about every pain, every symptom, everything. They had the best doctor-patient relationship. Whenever she would go to take her treatments, Dr. Robertson would always examine her. He was very concerned about her gaining weight. She attributed it to Jesse's good cooking. They both laughed. He told her that he wanted to do a com- plete physical. Tiger started to fuss but agreed. She told Dr. Robertson that she would be waiting for his telephone call to tell her that she was okay.

Two days later Dr. Robertson called. Tiger began talk- ing to him about everything. Dr. Robertson listened. He interrupted her to tell her that he had some news for her. Tiger immediately became frightened, because she thought that he was going to tell her that she had less time to live. He told her that she was pregnant. There was a moment of silence on the telephone and then Tiger laughed. She told him that all her life she had heard that it took nine months to have a baby. She told him that she would not even be alive to have the baby. Dr. Robertson said he would see what would happen. He told her that maybe she had more time. Tiger became very angry with him. She told him that she did not think that this was a time to joke with her about her life. She felt that she would have to terminate the pregnancy based on her condition. Dr. Robertson said that he wanted to talk to her and Jesse before a decision was made.

Jesse and Tiger arrived at the doctor's office about 9:00 that morning. Jesse was so excited. He told Dr. Robertson that God had answered his prayer. Tiger looked at both of them and asked what were the next steps in resolving the problem. Dr. Robertson and Jesse both agreed that Tiger could have the baby. Tiger looked at both of them and wept. She told Jesse that she would do anything for him, but this was impossible. She reminded both of them that she was dying. Dr. Robertson said it was a great possibility that she had more months and even more years to live. Tiger thought both of them had lost their minds. She embraced Jesse and told him how sorry she was that she could not have the baby.

Jesse asked her to do it for him. She informed him that if she did have the baby that her body was so frail that he could lose her and the baby in the delivery room. Jesse told her to let him and God worry about that. She told him that she had never had a baby and that her age would be a factor also. Jesse begged her to give this a chance. Tiger finally said okay. She told both of them that she would try, but she knew she would die even earlier in this process. Dr. Robertson assured her that this was a delicate situation, but he would be there every step of the way.

Tiger had an easy pregnancy. She had no complications. Dr. Robertson and Jesse were there every step of the way.

The nurses would ask Dr. Robertson if he was sure it was not his baby. He just could not believe that Tiger actually lived to have a seven pound baby boy. Tiger did not ask for any additional medication. She only wanted Jesse in her room. She thought that if she had the baby that she would die in the delivery room.

Dr. Robertson did not know what would happen during her pregnancy. He knew that Jesse was one of the most considerate husbands he had ever seen. He had consulted the best doctors he knew. He knew this was an interesting case. He was so happy for Jesse but sad, because similar to Tiger, he felt her life would end on the table. He wanted this so much for the both of them and for whatever reasons unexplainable to him. Tiger carried the baby full term, had a smooth delivery, and gave birth to a beautiful baby boy. The local newspaper captured everything. It was a miracle that Tiger lived to have her son. Tiger and Jesse were heroes and so was the baby. Tiger could not stop thanking Dr. Robertson and God for her beautiful son. She told Jesse that she knew she could depend on him for what time she had left. Jesse asked her not to talk about that but to enjoy their son. She agreed but she knew she had lived beyond her time and she knew death was getting closer and closer. She was happy that she had given Jesse a son. They named him Jesse Jerome Rogers, Jr. She could not believe that in her late forties with leukemia she had a healthy son. Dr. Robertson felt that her love for Jesse just caused her to soar beyond her illness.

Jesse Jr. was the love of their life. Tiger thought Jesse was going to give up training Buster. Jesse could not keep his eyes off their son. He brought so much joy to their lives. They would sit up and talk about how they did not think anything could make them any happier. Tiger and Jesse wondered what took them so long to meet. Tiger could not believe it and her mother fussed about her waiting so long to give her a grandchild. She never understood why she did not have any children by Wilbur. Tiger wrote down everything Jesse Jr. did. She knew she would not be around because the pains were getting worse; she wanted Jesse to be able to tell him about different things he did as a baby. Tiger would get sad sometimes because she knew she would have to leave her two men behind. Tiger prayed more after having Jesse Jr. in her life. She would talk to God and just ask Him to make Jesse and Jesse Jr.'s lives easy. She asked God to allow Jesse to find a woman who would love him and her son the way she did. She would tell God that she thought this love that she felt was only in romance novels or on television, but it was real.

Dr. Robertson was amazed that Tiger had reached her forty-seventh birthday. Jesse threw the biggest surprise party ever and in planning this party, he knew that Tiger would leave him soon. She was growing weaker and Ms. Lisa came by on a regular basis to help take care of Jesse Jr. He was almost one year old and he adored his mother. Jesse had tried to talk to him about his mother but he knew he did not understand. Jesse Jr. would look at him smiling just like he understood everything he was trying to say. Jesse would just hold him and cry.

Tiger was surprised and she was the most beautiful woman at the party. She hugged all of her friends and told them that she was the happiest woman in the world. She told them how much she loved Jesse and Jesse Jr. and when the time was right she would go, but truly her life had been fulfilled. Jesse could not keep his eyes off his wife that night. He watched every move she made. Ms. Lisa brought Jesse Jr. in a couple of times, but everyone knew it was past his bedtime. Tiger handled him so gently. Watching her with her son was so beautiful. Jesse loved to see them together and her interacting with him.

After the party, Tiger and Jesse made love as if it was the first time. Tiger seemed as if she had gained her strength back. Both knew that this was truly a moment that they had to cherish. Her illness had caused them not to spend as much time together. She was in more pain and Jesse was very sensitive to her.

Tiger grew weaker and Jesse Jr. moved in the basement with Ms. Lisa. He had everything down there. Ms. Lisa would let Tiger hold him when she felt strong enough. He would kiss her and it seemed as if he was telling her how much he loved her. Seeing them together would bring tears to Ms. Lisa's eyes. Ms. Lisa and Tiger became close friends. She talked to her about everything. She even told Ms. Lisa about how she wanted her funeral. She said that she want-ed to tell her because it was so difficult for Jesse. She would encourage him to go train Buster. Buster had won some mi-nor fights and she was so happy. She was happy that that kept Jesse's mind off of her. He would call her when he got to the gym and when he was on his way. Sometimes Jesse would call her in the car when he drove in the yard. Jesse was too much, but she loved everything about this young man.

She knew Jesse loved her. Almost every afternoon she would cry because she could feel the time getting near. It was hard for her to get out of bed. Dr. Robertson had sug-gested several places for her to go, but she wanted to stay home with Jesse and Jesse Jr. Ms. Lisa took care of her and Jesse Jr. Tiger would write in her journal every night so that when Jesse Jr. got older he would always have her thoughts with him.

Jesse felt it was time to stop his training and stay home with Tiger, but she would not hear of that. She wanted him to continue every thing just like nothing was happening. She reminded him of the good money they were paying Ms. Lisa. She was a great babysitter. She wished him well and told him that Buster would become his champion. She loved Buster. He had become a son to her. She wanted him to do something constructive with his life and she knew Jesse would make that possible.

Jesse left that morning knowing that Tiger was not well and so weak. She insisted that he go to work. Jesse begged her several time to let him stay home with her. She told him no. She knew Buster's boxing career was important. This was the day he had to box and she did not want him or Jesse to miss the match. She told Jesse to keep his mind on what he was doing. She told him that she would be okay. She promised him that she would be in good hands no matter what. He decided to go and left feeling different than ever before. He didn't know what he was feeling. He wasn't sure if Tiger was telling him goodbye or if Buster was going to lose the fight. He kissed her passionately and told her that he would be back as soon as possible. She smiled and told him to take care of Jesse Jr. and Buster.

Tiger called the hospital as soon as Jesse left. She talked quietly on the telephone so Ms. Lisa would not hear her conversation. She knew that she was in her final hours. She called her mother and in her conversation she thanked her and said goodbye. She asked Dr. Robertson to send a cab for her to come to the hospital. He immediately called the cab company and had one of their drivers to pick her up. She was so weak, but she yelled downstairs to have Ms. Lisa bring Jesse Jr. up to see her. Ms. Lisa walked up the steps shaking and feeling that Tiger would not be with them long. She held back her tears as she gave Jesse Jr. to his mother. Tiger pulled herself together, played with Jesse Jr., and kissed him. She told him that she loved him and no matter what she never regretted the day he was born nor the day she met his father. Tiger told Ms. Lisa to help her get dressed, because Dr. Robertson was sending a cab to pick her up. She told Ms. Lisa that Dr. Robertson wanted to run some tests. Ms. Lisa was a bit puzzled because she knew that Tiger did not have a scheduled doctor's appointment. She did not say anything. She helped Tiger get dressed.

The cab driver called the house. Tiger was dressed. She hugged and thanked Ms. Lisa for helping her and for helping her with her son. Ms. Lisa turned away to hold back her tears. She told Tiger that she had become the daughter she never had. Tiger laughed and told her that she was her mother away from home. As they were embracing, Otis knocked on the door. He told Tiger that he was there to pick her up. Tiger knew Otis. They were in first grade together. He knew she was sick and he had been there several time taking Tiger to and from the grocery store, pharmacy, and medical center.

Otis was quiet that morning. He always had a lot to talk about. Tiger sensed that he knew that she would not be around long. She asked Otis about his wife and children. He answered her and started talking about the weather. Later, he shared a Bible verse with her.

Dr. Robertson met her at the car. He thanked Otis. Otis told him that this trip was on him. He kissed Tiger on the cheek and told her that he would see her the next time. She told Dr. Robertson that she wanted to be in the hospital when she died. She asked him to call Ms. Lisa, Jesse, and her mother after everything was over. He smiled and asked her why didn't she want Jesse by her side. She said that she wanted him to keep his mind on his fight. He smiled and told her how much Jesse would want to be there. She agreed, but she asked if he would respect her wishes. Dr. Robertson did.

Around seven o'clock that afternoon Buster became the middle weight champion of the world. Jesse ran to the telephone to call Tiger. Ms. Lisa answered and said that Tiger went to the hospital earlier that day. She said that she had not heard anything, but she thought he was there with her. Jesse dropped the telephone and ran outside to get a cab to the hospital. He did not have time to get his car out of the parking garage. He talked to Ms. Lisa all the way there, asking her about Tiger and how she appeared when she left. Ms. Lisa gave him all the details.

Before the driver could make a complete stop, Jesse jumped out of the car and ran into the hospital. He asked for her room number and ran up four flights of stairs. He saw Dr. Robertson and asked where Tiger was. He told her that he knew she only had minutes to live. Jesse ran in and held her in his arms. Tiger looked at Jesse smiled and said, "I will always love you." He told her he won the fight. Tiger smiled, grabbed his hand, and died.

Jesse walked back into his house that night so empty. Ms. Lisa grabbed him and held him tightly. She told him that everything would be alright. He looked at her and told her how much he loved Tiger. Ms. Lisa nodded her head in agreement. She handed Jesse a note that she found after Tiger left for the hospital.

Jesse read the note and it said, "You were the best thing that ever happened to me. Thank you for being my husband, lover, and friend, and most of all, thank you for our son. No matter what you do and where you go, you will always be my distant lover."

The End

Contact Information

Mable I. Cox
Post Office Box 441035
Fort Washington, MD 20749

(301) 412-7615
beeyou5@gmail.com

CPSIA information can be obtained at www.ICGtesting.com
Printed in the USA
BVOW020402230512

290733BV00007B/2/P